WITHDRAWN

HAUNTED HISTORY

CURSE OF THE EGYPTIAN PRINCESS

by K.C. Kelley

Illustrations by Lisa Naffziger

BEARPORT PUBLISHING

Minneapolis, Minnesota

BEAR CLAW

Credits

Cover art by Candy Briones.
Interior coloring by Eva Andrews.
Photos: 22T: David Bjorgen/Wikimedia; 22B: Thilo Parg/Wikimedia

Bearport Publishing
Minneapolis, MN
President: Jen Jenson
Director of Product Development: Spencer Brinker
Editor: Allison Juda

Produced by Shoreline Publishing Group LLC
Santa Barbara, California
Designer: Patty Kelley
Editorial Director: James Buckley Jr.

DISCLAIMER: This graphic story is a dramatization based on true events. It is intended to give the reader a sense of the narrative rather than a presentation of actual details as they occurred.

Library of Congress Cataloging-in-Publication Data

Names: Kelley, K. C., author. | Naffziger, Lisa, illustrator.
Title: Curse of the Egyptian princess / by K. C. Kelley ; illustrations by Lisa Naffziger.
Description: Bear Claw. | Minneapolis, Minnesota : Bearport Publishing Company, [2021] | Series: Haunted history | Includes bibliographical references and index.
Identifiers: LCCN 2020035418 (print) | LCCN 2020035419 (ebook) | ISBN 9781647475949 (library binding) | ISBN 9781647476021 (paperback) | ISBN 9781647476106 (ebook)
Subjects: CYAC: Mystery and detective stories. | Mummies–Fiction. | Blessing and cursing–Fiction. | Egypt–Antiquities–Fiction.
Classification: LCC PZ7.7.K445 Cu 2021 (print) | LCC PZ7.7.K445 (ebook) | DDC 741.5/973–dc23
LC record available at https://lccn.loc.gov/2020035418
LC ebook record available at https://lccn.loc.gov/2020035419

Copyright © 2021 Bearport Publishing Company. All rights reserved. No part of this publication may be reproduced in whole or in part, stored in any retrieval system, or transmitted in any form or by any means, electronic, mechanical, photocopying, recording, or otherwise, without written permission from the publisher.

For more information, write to Bearport Publishing, 5357 Penn Avenue South, Minneapolis, MN 55419. Printed in the United States of America.

CONTENTS

Mummies and Museums 4
Mummy Mania 6
The Curse Comes Home 10
The Curse Continues 18

Other Famous Curses 22
Glossary 23
Index 24
Read More 24
Learn More Online 24

MUMMIES AND MUSEUMS

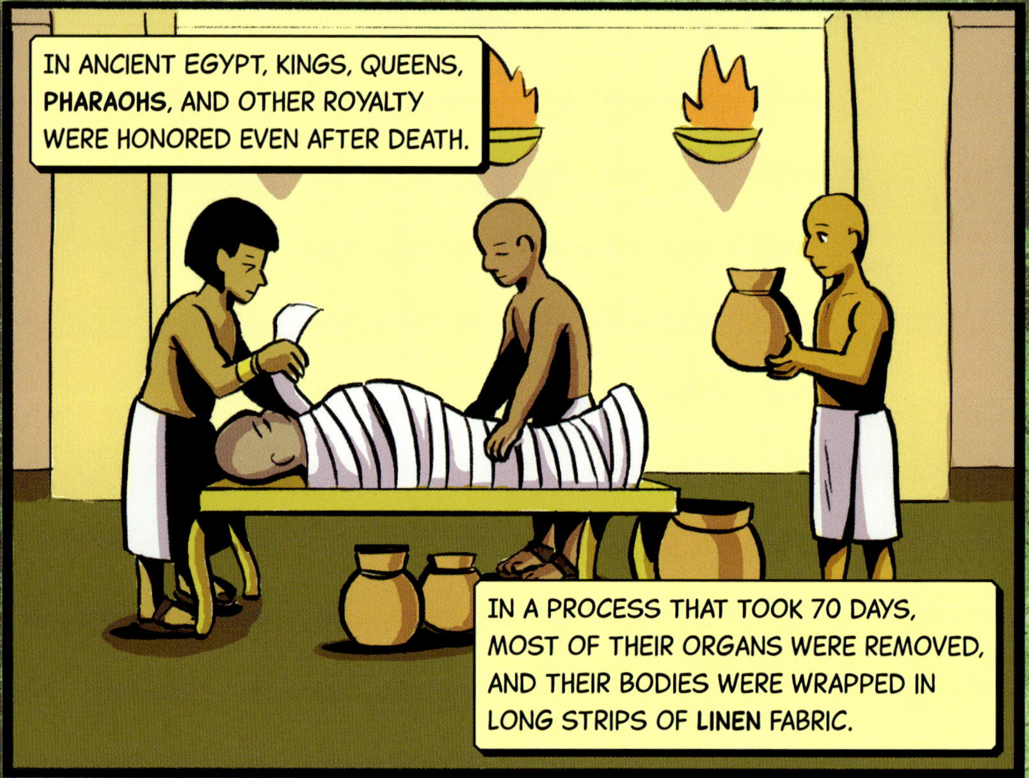
IN ANCIENT EGYPT, KINGS, QUEENS, **PHARAOHS**, AND OTHER ROYALTY WERE HONORED EVEN AFTER DEATH.
IN A PROCESS THAT TOOK 70 DAYS, MOST OF THEIR ORGANS WERE REMOVED, AND THEIR BODIES WERE WRAPPED IN LONG STRIPS OF **LINEN** FABRIC.

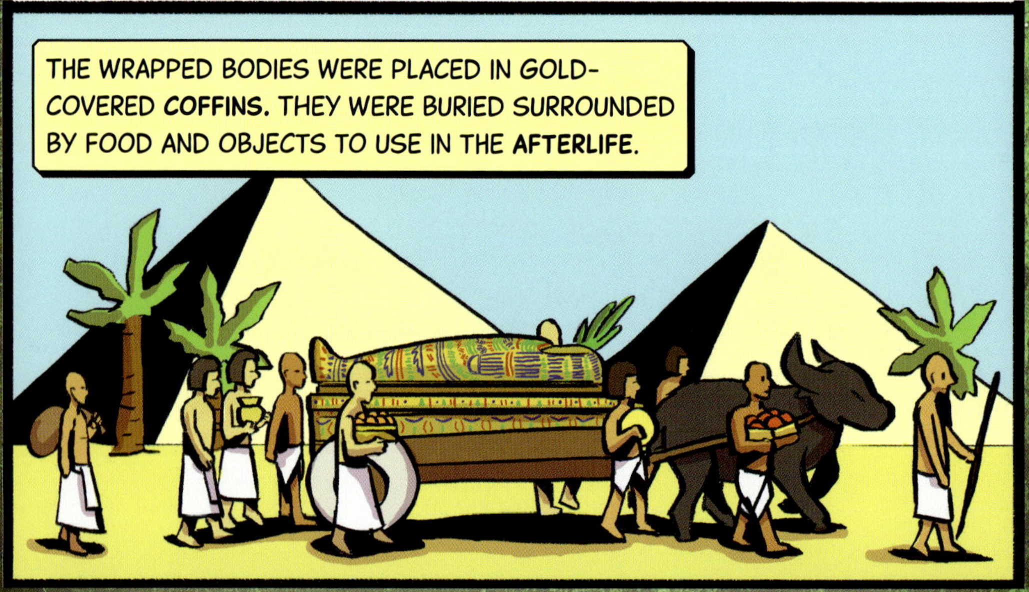
THE WRAPPED BODIES WERE PLACED IN GOLD-COVERED **COFFINS.** THEY WERE BURIED SURROUNDED BY FOOD AND OBJECTS TO USE IN THE **AFTERLIFE**.

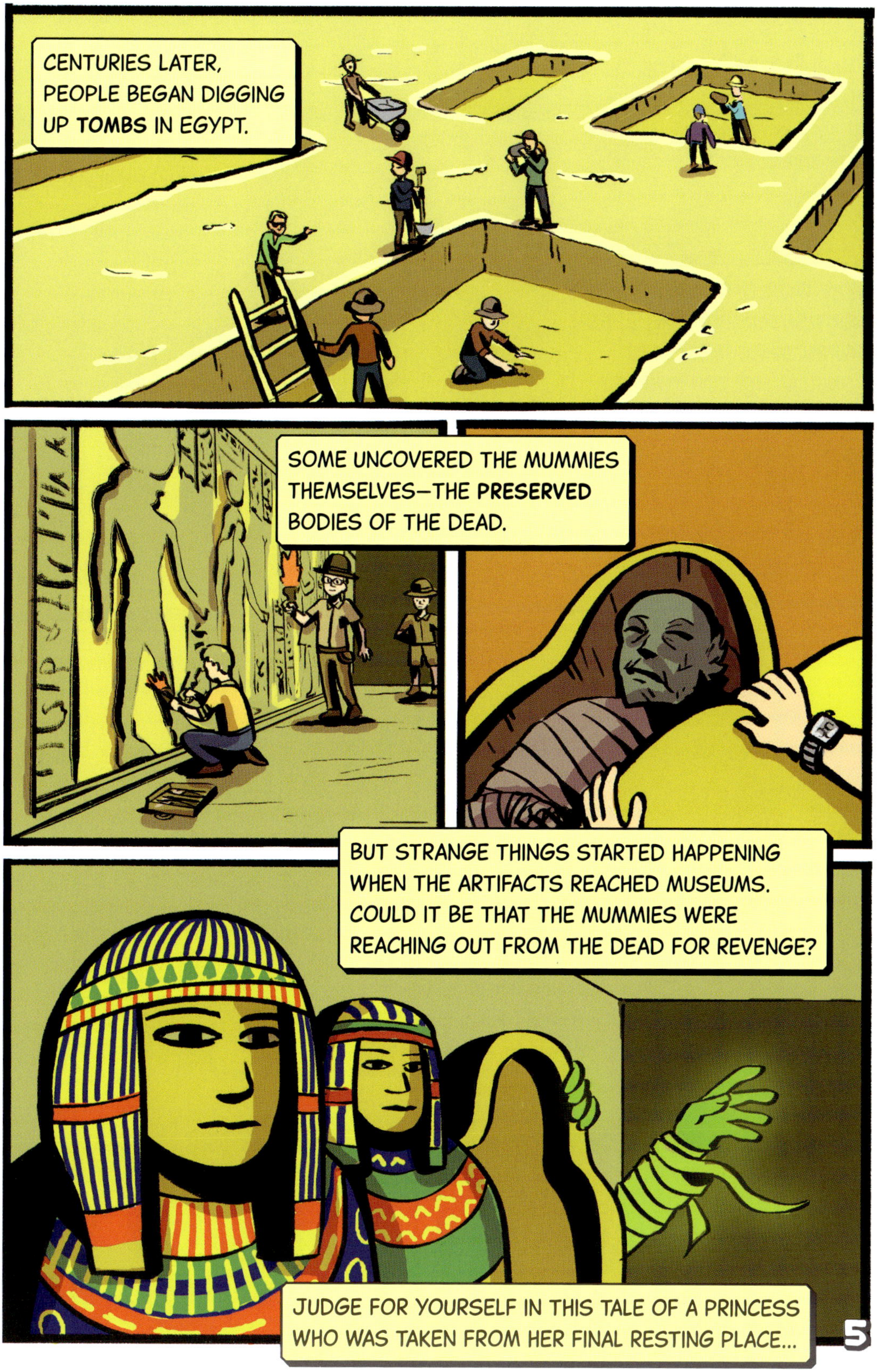
CENTURIES LATER, PEOPLE BEGAN DIGGING UP TOMBS IN EGYPT.
SOME UNCOVERED THE MUMMIES THEMSELVES—THE PRESERVED BODIES OF THE DEAD.
BUT STRANGE THINGS STARTED HAPPENING WHEN THE ARTIFACTS REACHED MUSEUMS. COULD IT BE THAT THE MUMMIES WERE REACHING OUT FROM THE DEAD FOR REVENGE?
JUDGE FOR YOURSELF IN THIS TALE OF A PRINCESS WHO WAS TAKEN FROM HER FINAL RESTING PLACE...

MUMMY MANIA

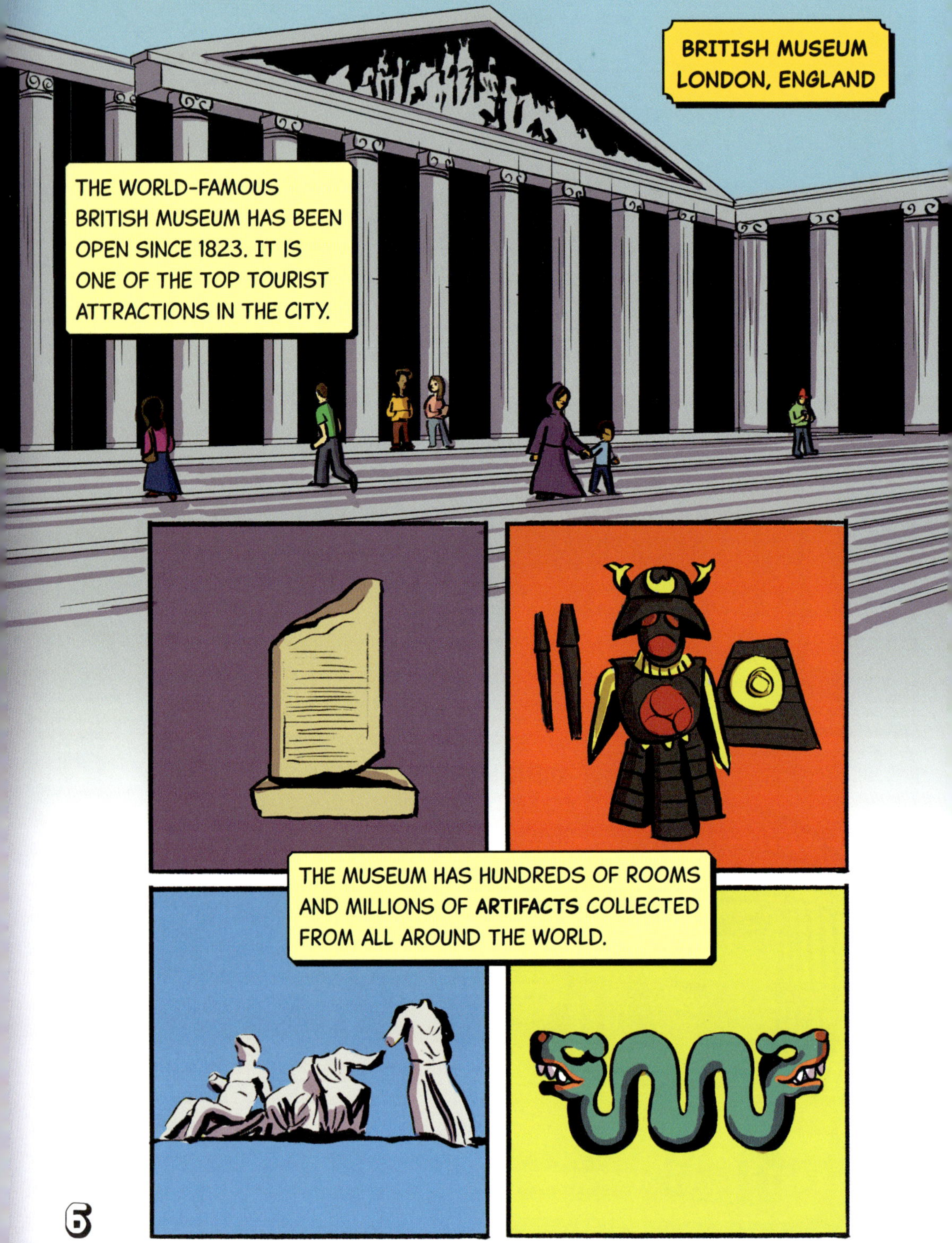
BRITISH MUSEUM
LONDON, ENGLAND
THE WORLD-FAMOUS BRITISH MUSEUM HAS BEEN OPEN SINCE 1823. IT IS ONE OF THE TOP TOURIST ATTRACTIONS IN THE CITY.
THE MUSEUM HAS HUNDREDS OF ROOMS AND MILLIONS OF **ARTIFACTS** COLLECTED FROM ALL AROUND THE WORLD.

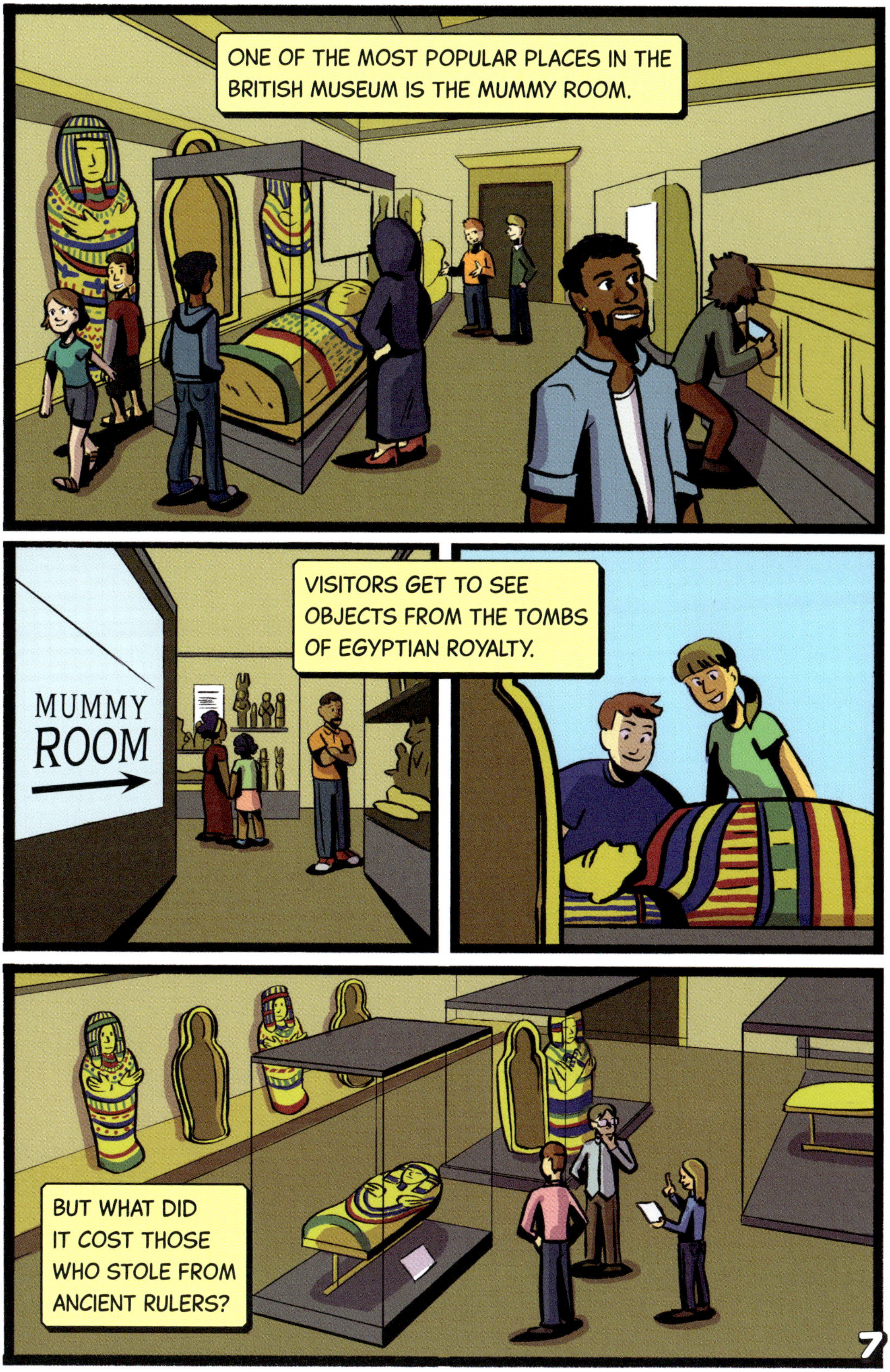
ONE OF THE MOST POPULAR PLACES IN THE BRITISH MUSEUM IS THE MUMMY ROOM.
MUMMY ROOM
VISITORS GET TO SEE OBJECTS FROM THE TOMBS OF EGYPTIAN ROYALTY.
BUT WHAT DID IT COST THOSE WHO STOLE FROM ANCIENT RULERS?

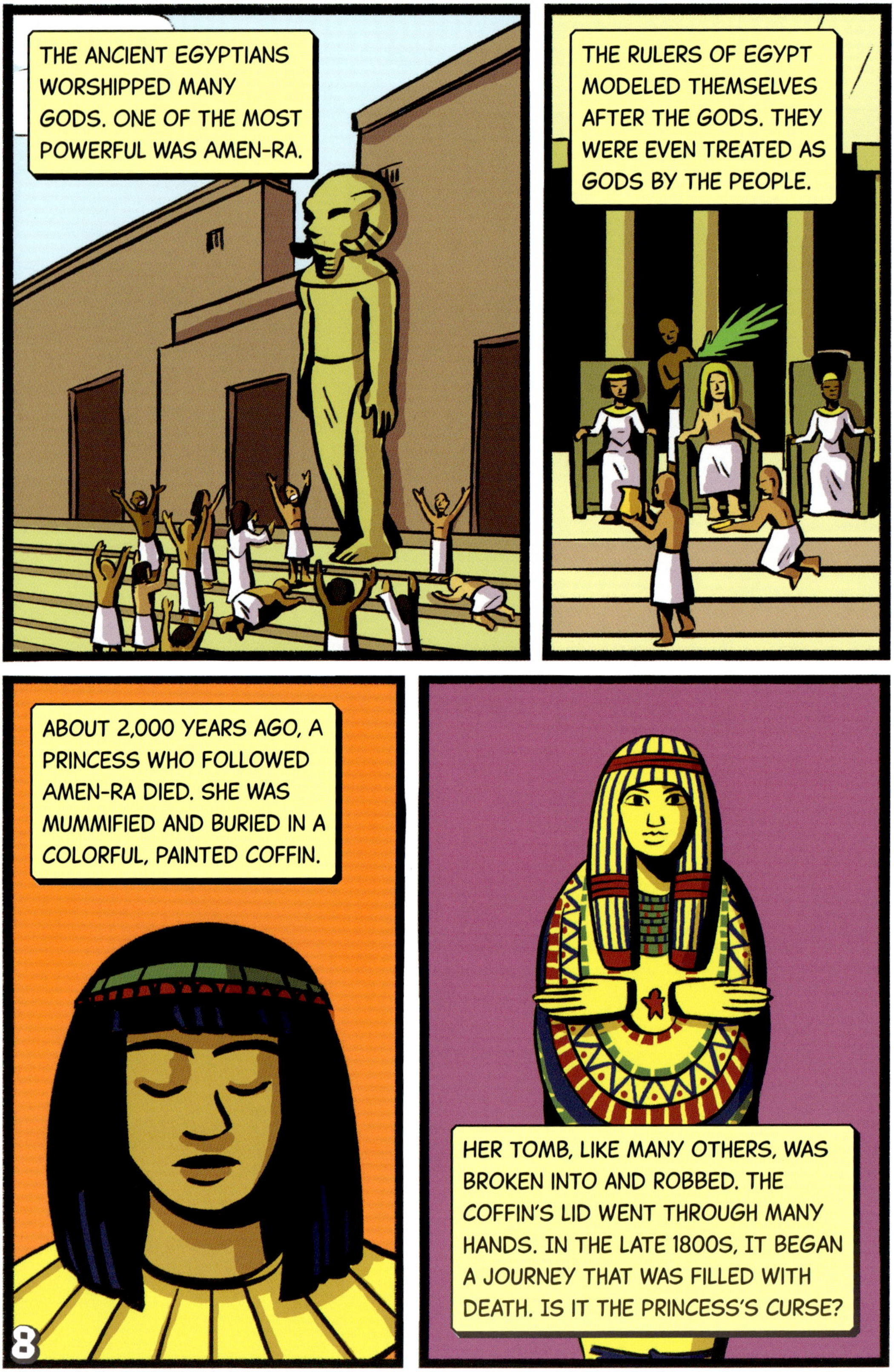
THE ANCIENT EGYPTIANS WORSHIPPED MANY GODS. ONE OF THE MOST POWERFUL WAS AMEN-RA.
THE RULERS OF EGYPT MODELED THEMSELVES AFTER THE GODS. THEY WERE EVEN TREATED AS GODS BY THE PEOPLE.
ABOUT 2,000 YEARS AGO, A PRINCESS WHO FOLLOWED AMEN-RA DIED. SHE WAS MUMMIFIED AND BURIED IN A COLORFUL, PAINTED COFFIN.
HER TOMB, LIKE MANY OTHERS, WAS BROKEN INTO AND ROBBED. THE COFFIN'S LID WENT THROUGH MANY HANDS. IN THE LATE 1800S, IT BEGAN A JOURNEY THAT WAS FILLED WITH DEATH. IS IT THE PRINCESS'S CURSE?

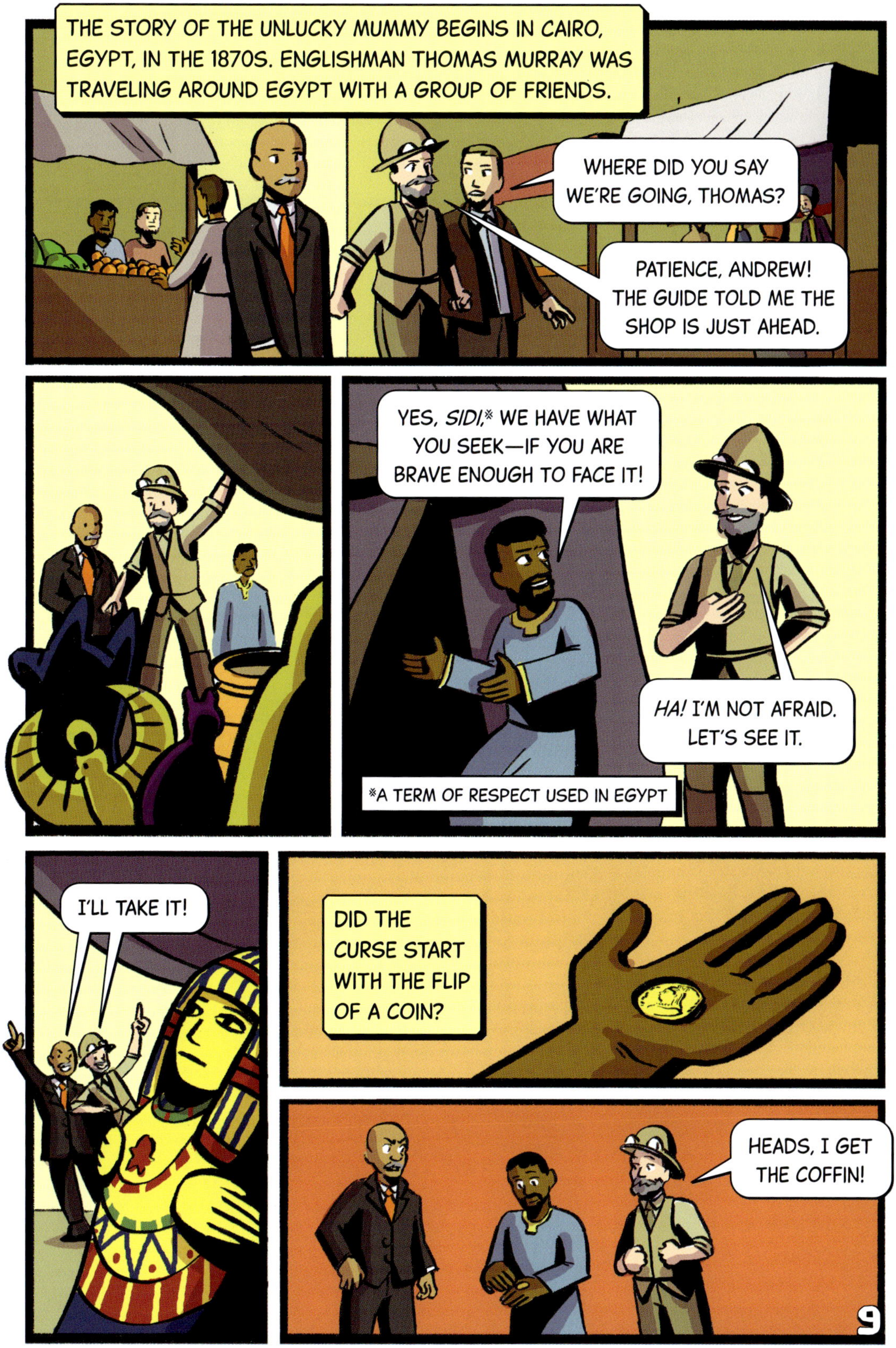
THE STORY OF THE UNLUCKY MUMMY BEGINS IN CAIRO, EGYPT, IN THE 1870S. ENGLISHMAN THOMAS MURRAY WAS TRAVELING AROUND EGYPT WITH A GROUP OF FRIENDS.
WHERE DID YOU SAY WE'RE GOING, THOMAS?
PATIENCE, ANDREW! THE GUIDE TOLD ME THE SHOP IS JUST AHEAD.
YES, *SIDI*,* WE HAVE WHAT YOU SEEK—IF YOU ARE BRAVE ENOUGH TO FACE IT!
HA! I'M NOT AFRAID. LET'S SEE IT.
*A TERM OF RESPECT USED IN EGYPT
I'LL TAKE IT!
DID THE CURSE START WITH THE FLIP OF A COIN?
HEADS, I GET THE COFFIN!

THE CURSE COMES HOME

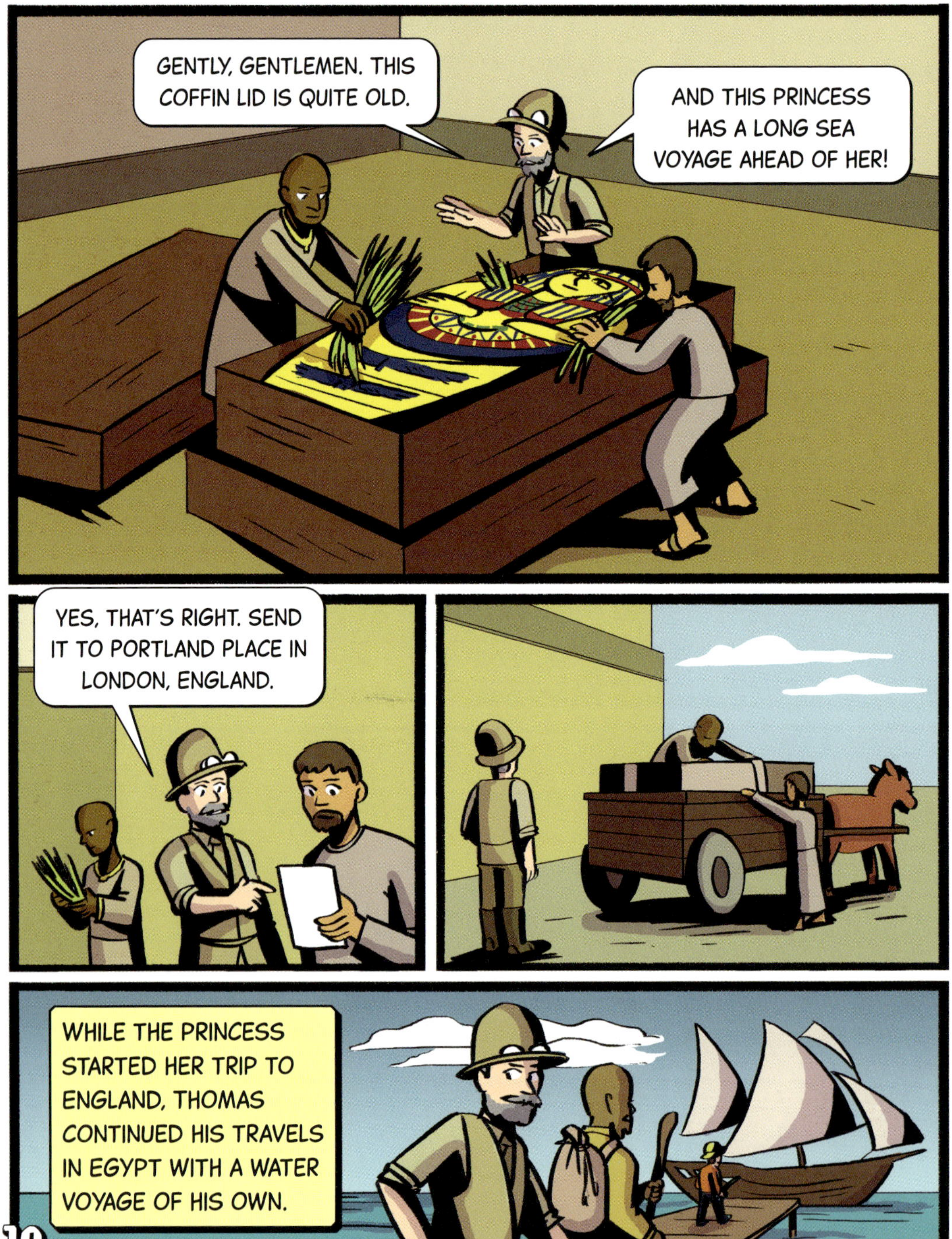
GENTLY, GENTLEMEN. THIS COFFIN LID IS QUITE OLD.
AND THIS PRINCESS HAS A LONG SEA VOYAGE AHEAD OF HER!
YES, THAT'S RIGHT. SEND IT TO PORTLAND PLACE IN LONDON, ENGLAND.
WHILE THE PRINCESS STARTED HER TRIP TO ENGLAND, THOMAS CONTINUED HIS TRAVELS IN EGYPT WITH A WATER VOYAGE OF HIS OWN.

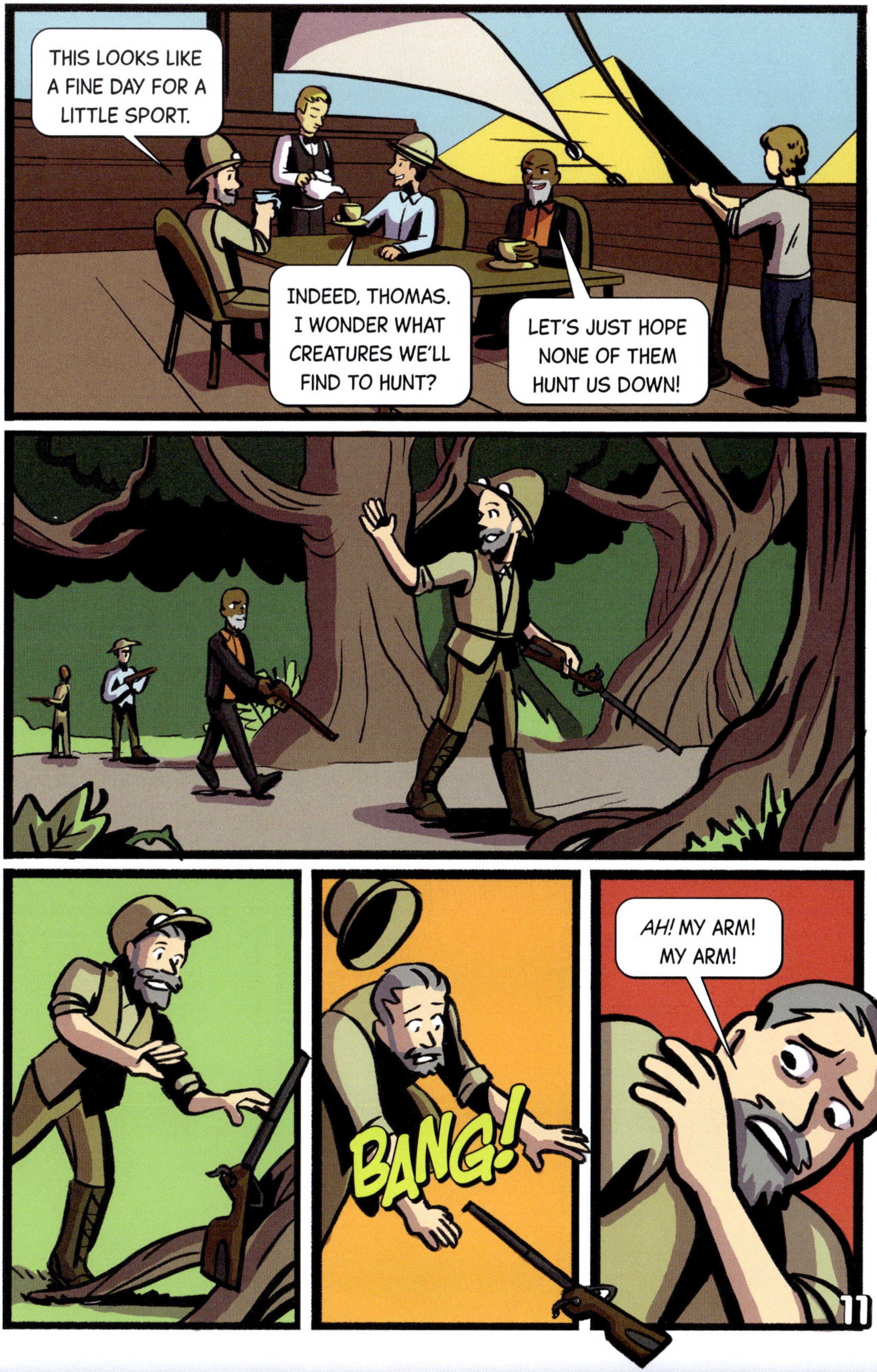
THIS LOOKS LIKE A FINE DAY FOR A LITTLE SPORT.
INDEED, THOMAS. I WONDER WHAT CREATURES WE'LL FIND TO HUNT?
LET'S JUST HOPE NONE OF THEM HUNT US DOWN!
BANG!
AH! MY ARM! MY ARM!

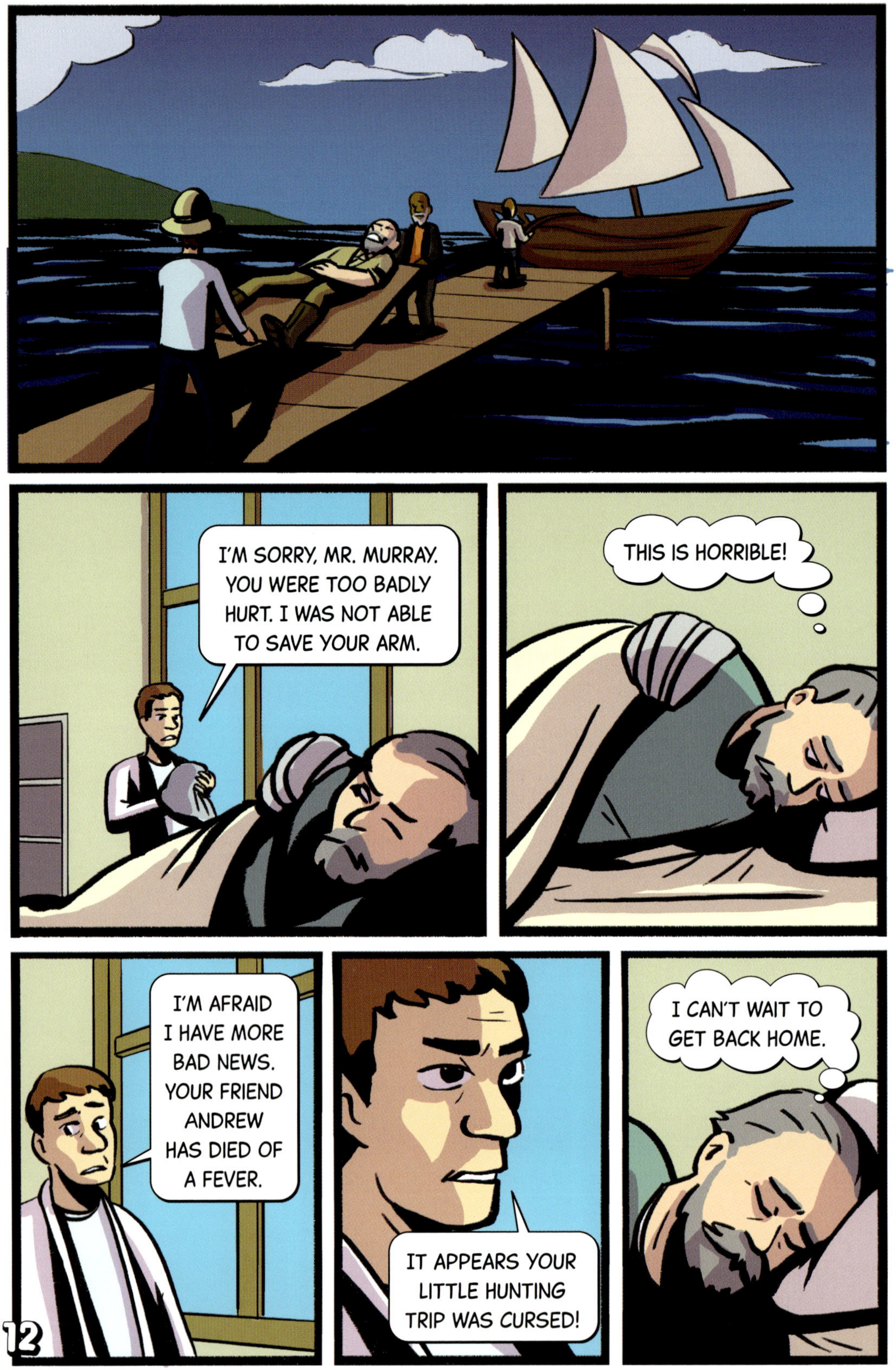
I'M SORRY, MR. MURRAY. YOU WERE TOO BADLY HURT. I WAS NOT ABLE TO SAVE YOUR ARM.
THIS IS HORRIBLE!
I'M AFRAID I HAVE MORE BAD NEWS. YOUR FRIEND ANDREW HAS DIED OF A FEVER.
IT APPEARS YOUR LITTLE HUNTING TRIP WAS CURSED!
I CAN'T WAIT TO GET BACK HOME.

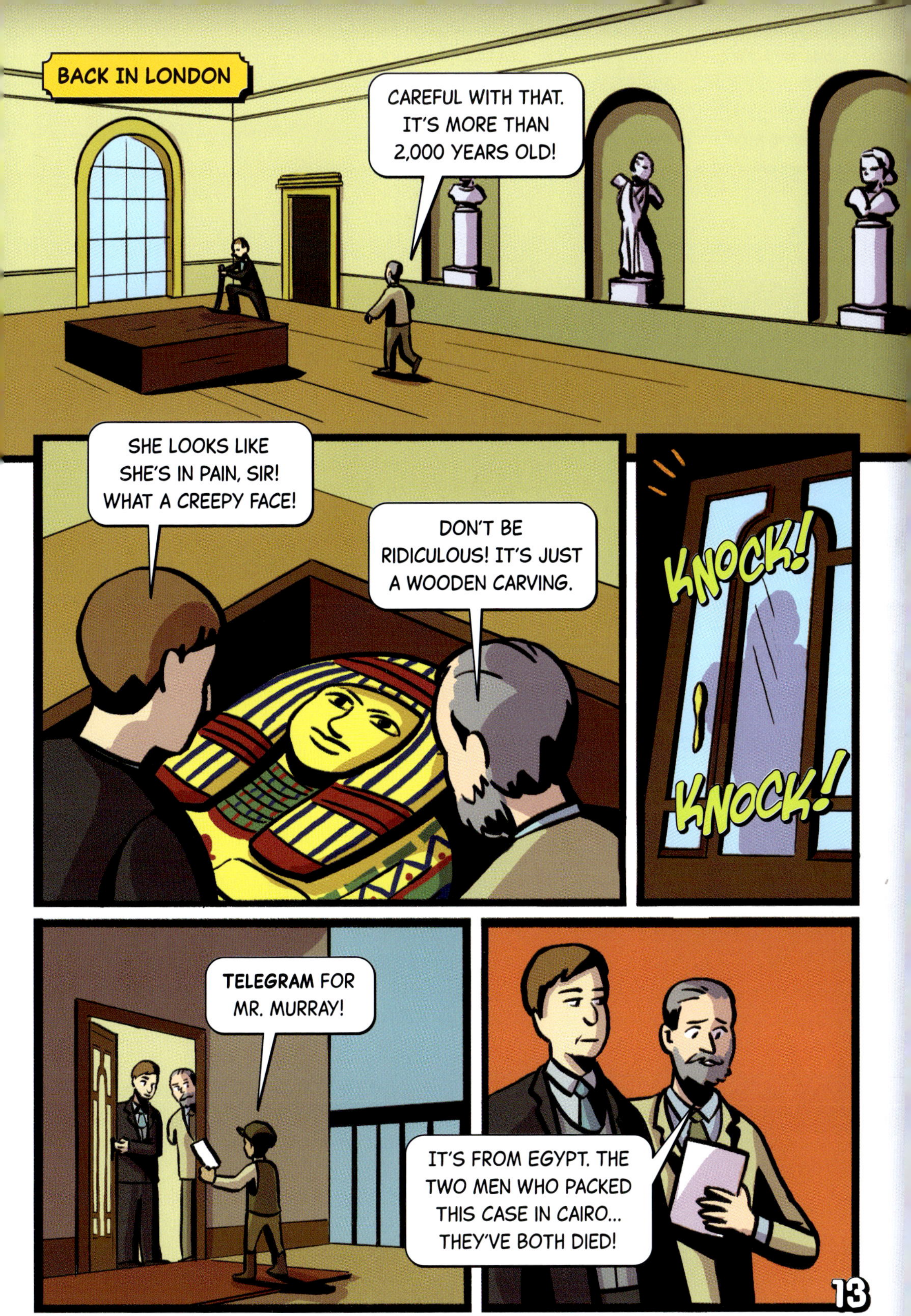
BACK IN LONDON
CAREFUL WITH THAT. IT'S MORE THAN 2,000 YEARS OLD!
SHE LOOKS LIKE SHE'S IN PAIN, SIR! WHAT A CREEPY FACE!
DON'T BE RIDICULOUS! IT'S JUST A WOODEN CARVING.
KNOCK! KNOCK!
TELEGRAM FOR MR. MURRAY!
IT'S FROM EGYPT. THE TWO MEN WHO PACKED THIS CASE IN CAIRO... THEY'VE BOTH DIED!

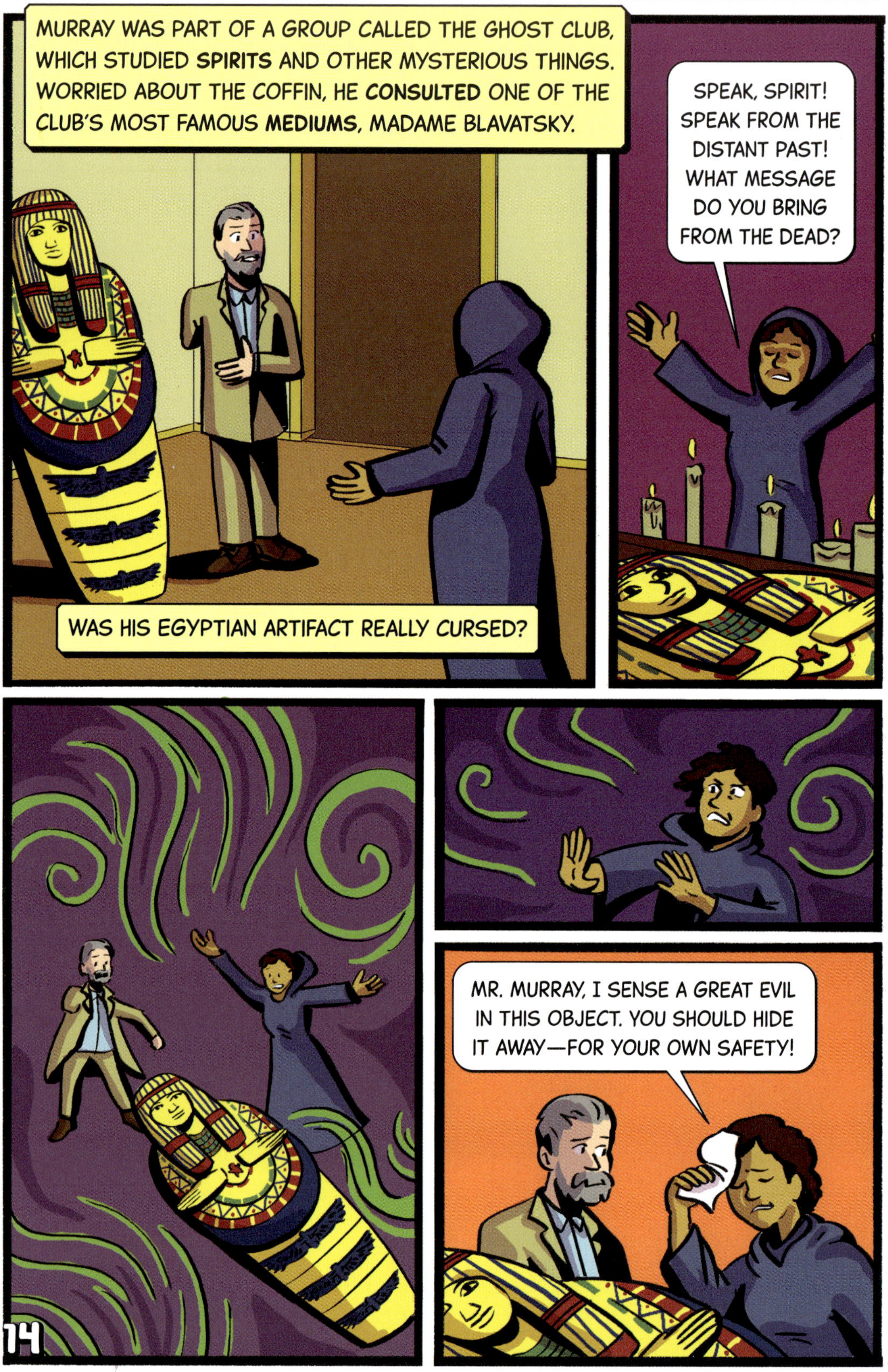
MURRAY WAS PART OF A GROUP CALLED THE GHOST CLUB, WHICH STUDIED **SPIRITS** AND OTHER MYSTERIOUS THINGS. WORRIED ABOUT THE COFFIN, HE **CONSULTED** ONE OF THE CLUB'S MOST FAMOUS **MEDIUMS**, MADAME BLAVATSKY.
WAS HIS EGYPTIAN ARTIFACT REALLY CURSED?
SPEAK, SPIRIT! SPEAK FROM THE DISTANT PAST! WHAT MESSAGE DO YOU BRING FROM THE DEAD?
MR. MURRAY, I SENSE A GREAT EVIL IN THIS OBJECT. YOU SHOULD HIDE IT AWAY—FOR YOUR OWN SAFETY!

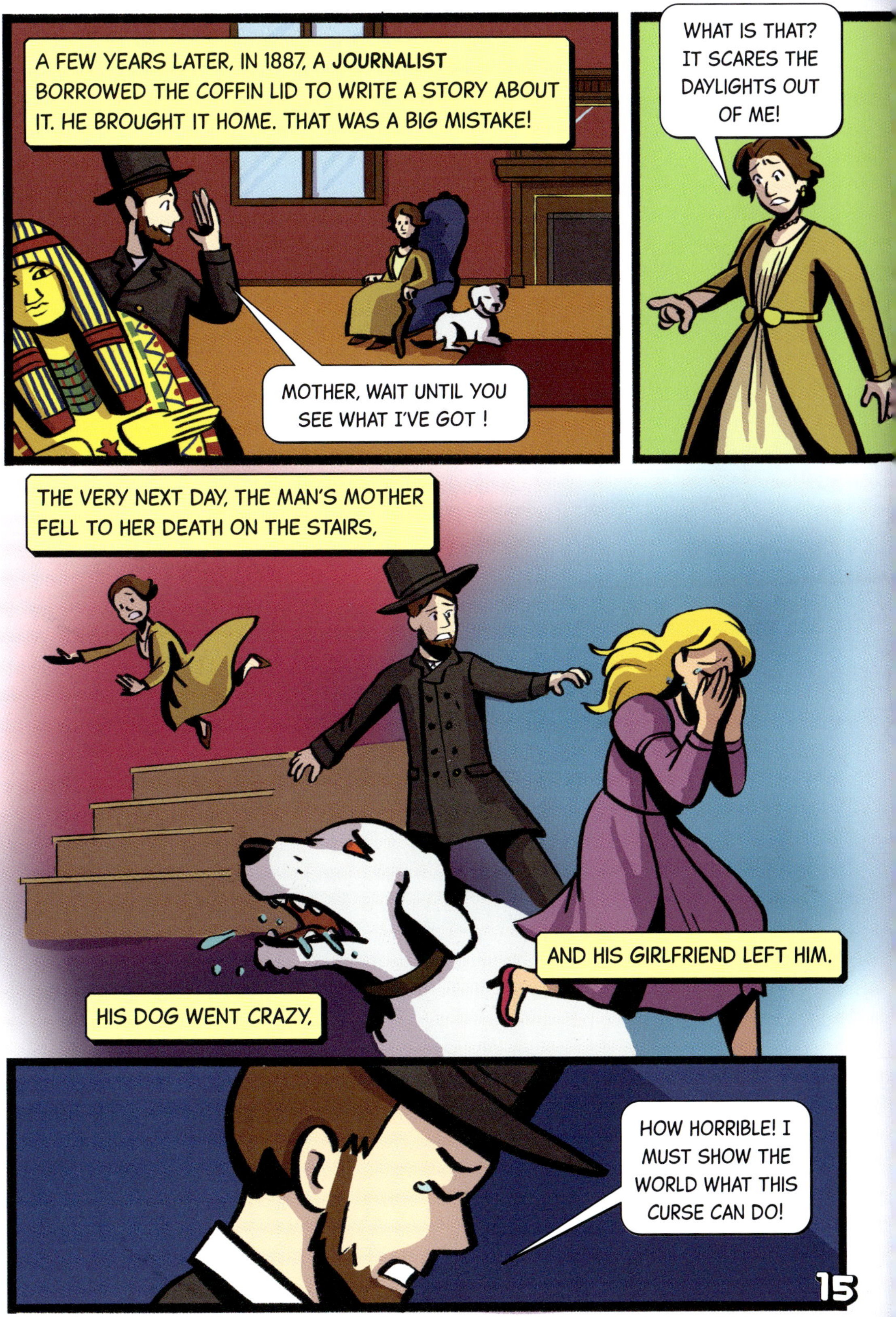

A FEW YEARS LATER, IN 1887, A **JOURNALIST** BORROWED THE COFFIN LID TO WRITE A STORY ABOUT IT. HE BROUGHT IT HOME. THAT WAS A BIG MISTAKE!
MOTHER, WAIT UNTIL YOU SEE WHAT I'VE GOT !
WHAT IS THAT? IT SCARES THE DAYLIGHTS OUT OF ME!
THE VERY NEXT DAY, THE MAN'S MOTHER FELL TO HER DEATH ON THE STAIRS,
HIS DOG WENT CRAZY,
AND HIS GIRLFRIEND LEFT HIM.
HOW HORRIBLE! I MUST SHOW THE WORLD WHAT THIS CURSE CAN DO!

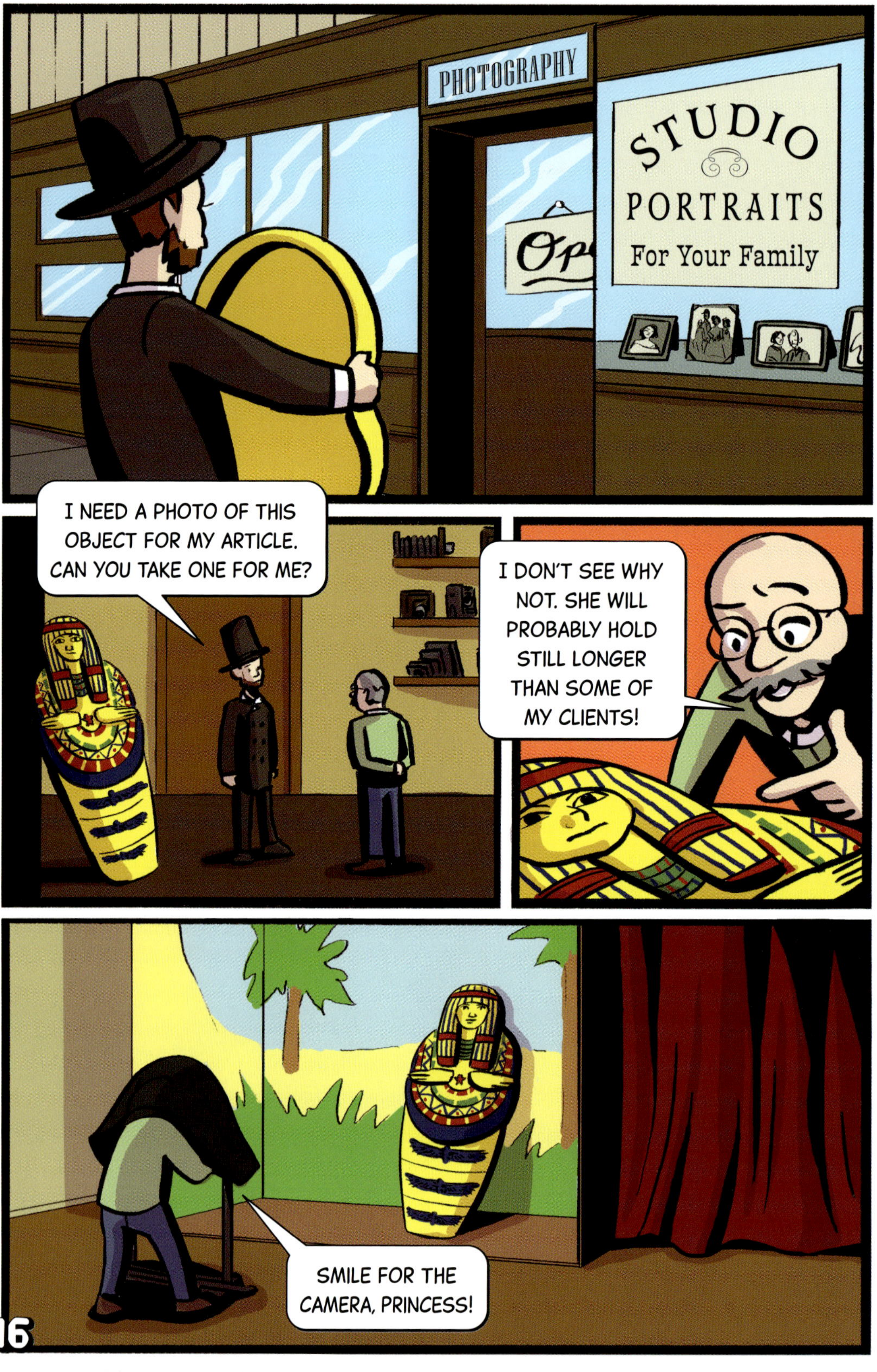
PHOTOGRAPHY
STUDIO
PORTRAITS
For Your Family
I NEED A PHOTO OF THIS OBJECT FOR MY ARTICLE. CAN YOU TAKE ONE FOR ME?
I DON'T SEE WHY NOT. SHE WILL PROBABLY HOLD STILL LONGER THAN SOME OF MY CLIENTS!
SMILE FOR THE CAMERA, PRINCESS!

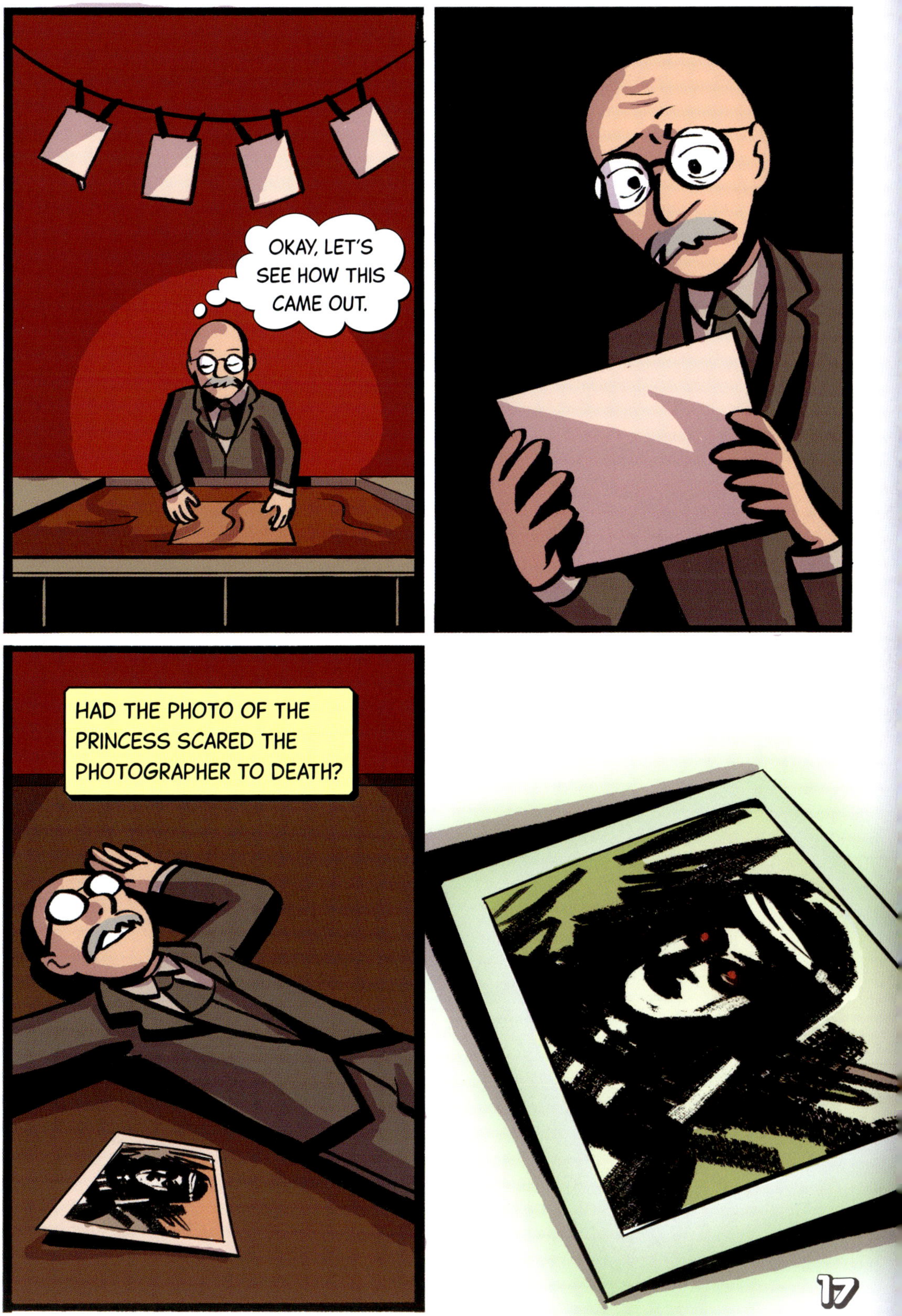
OKAY, LET'S SEE HOW THIS CAME OUT.
HAD THE PHOTO OF THE PRINCESS SCARED THE PHOTOGRAPHER TO DEATH?

THE CURSE CONTINUES

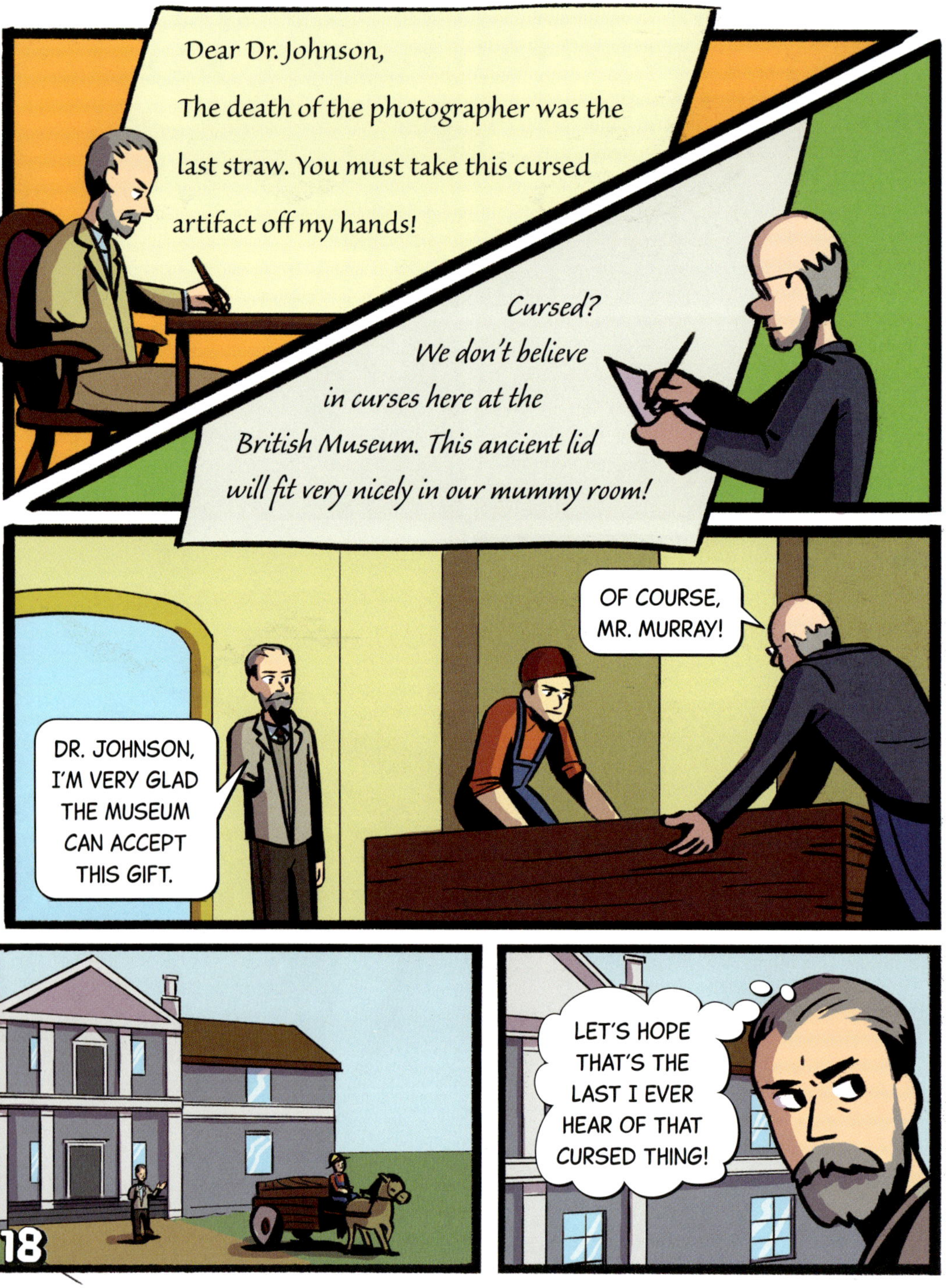
Dear Dr. Johnson,
The death of the photographer was the last straw. You must take this cursed artifact off my hands!
Cursed? We don't believe in curses here at the British Museum. This ancient lid will fit very nicely in our mummy room!
DR. JOHNSON, I'M VERY GLAD THE MUSEUM CAN ACCEPT THIS GIFT.
OF COURSE, MR. MURRAY!
LET'S HOPE THAT'S THE LAST I EVER HEAR OF THAT CURSED THING!

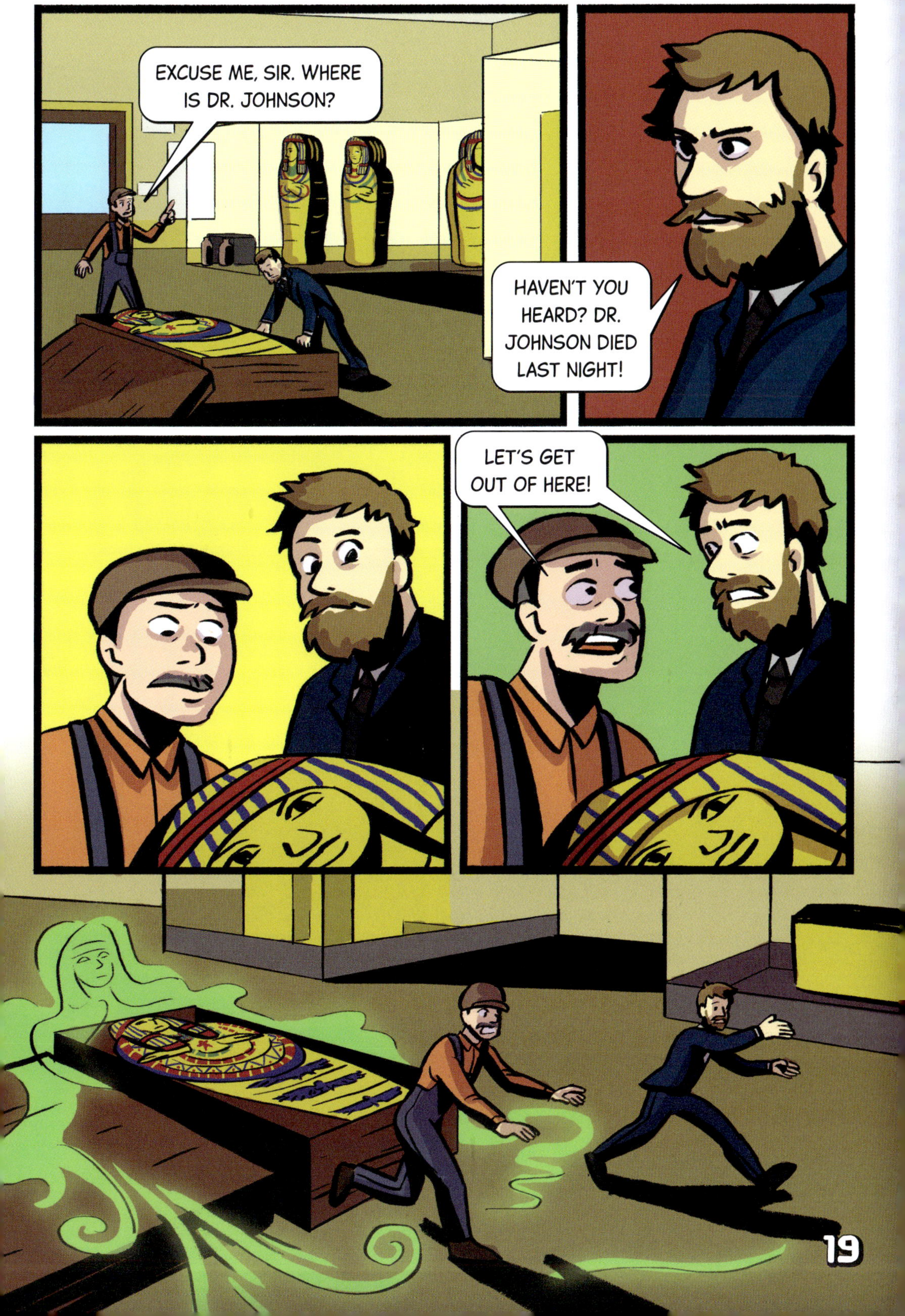
EXCUSE ME, SIR. WHERE IS DR. JOHNSON?
HAVEN'T YOU HEARD? DR. JOHNSON DIED LAST NIGHT!
LET'S GET OUT OF HERE!

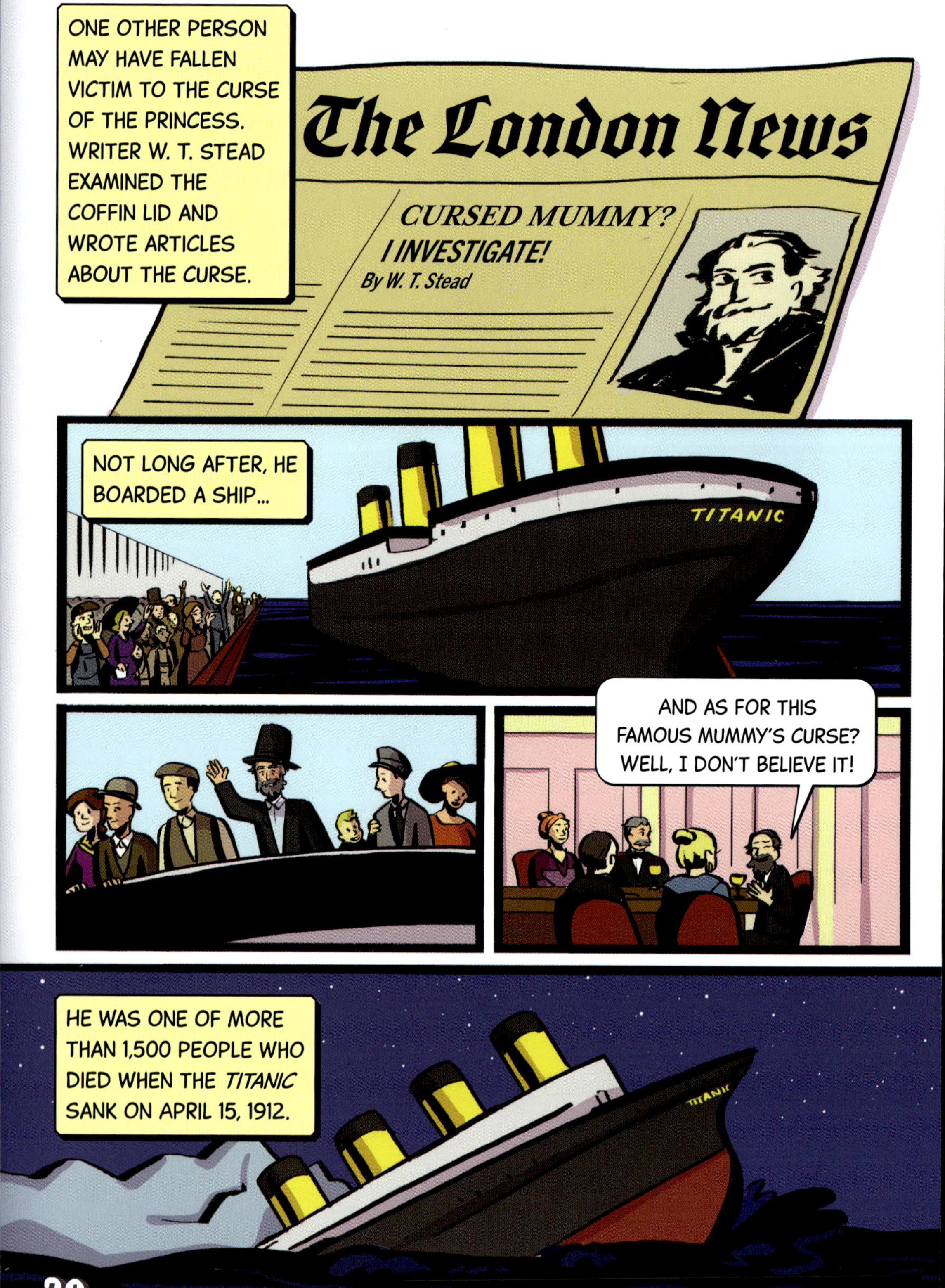

ONE OTHER PERSON MAY HAVE FALLEN VICTIM TO THE CURSE OF THE PRINCESS. WRITER W. T. STEAD EXAMINED THE COFFIN LID AND WROTE ARTICLES ABOUT THE CURSE.
The London News
CURSED MUMMY? I INVESTIGATE!
By W. T. Stead
NOT LONG AFTER, HE BOARDED A SHIP...
TITANIC
AND AS FOR THIS FAMOUS MUMMY'S CURSE? WELL, I DON'T BELIEVE IT!
HE WAS ONE OF MORE THAN 1,500 PEOPLE WHO DIED WHEN THE *TITANIC* SANK ON APRIL 15, 1912.
TITANIC

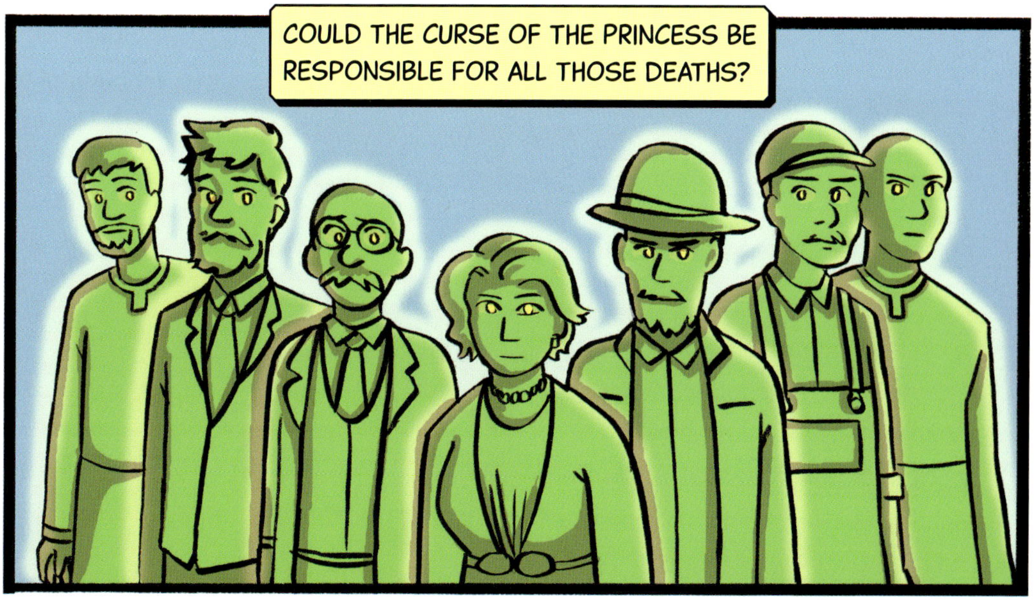
COULD THE CURSE OF THE PRINCESS BE RESPONSIBLE FOR ALL THOSE DEATHS?

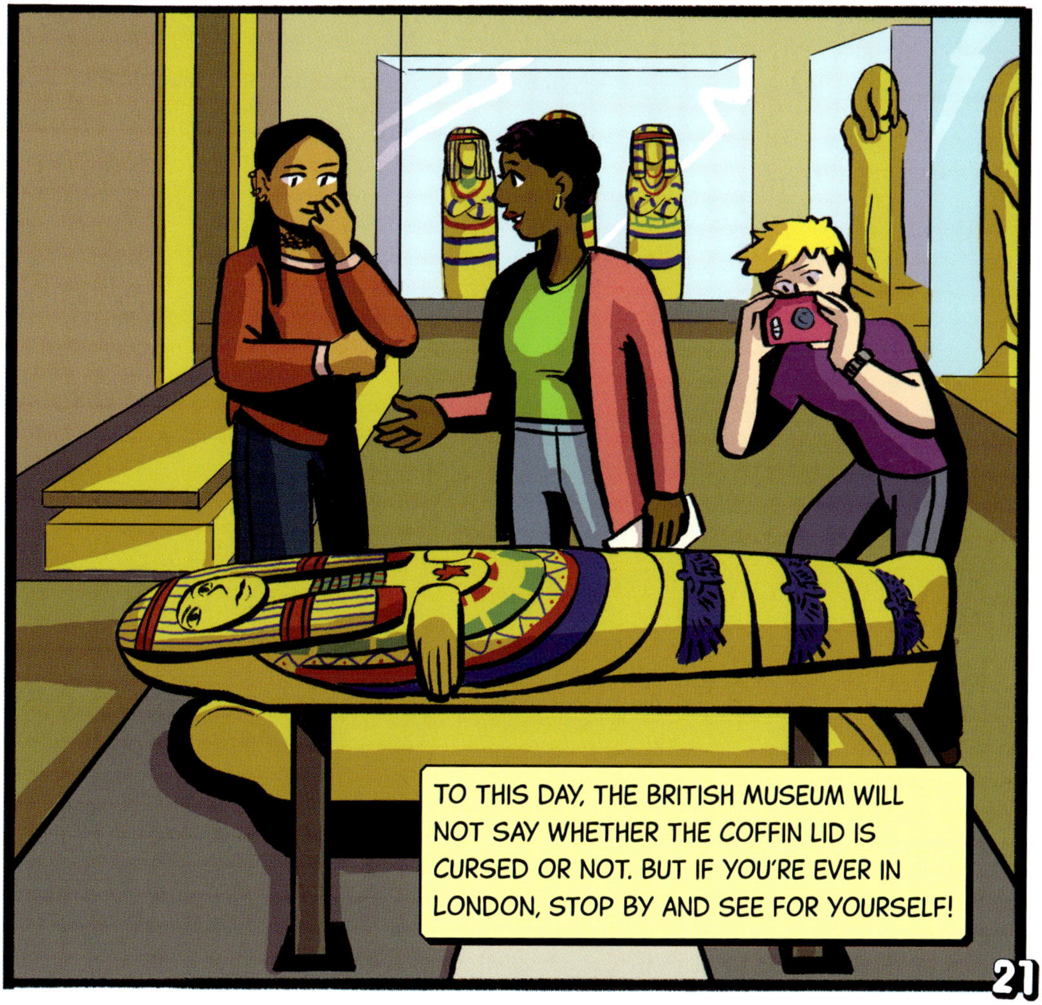
TO THIS DAY, THE BRITISH MUSEUM WILL NOT SAY WHETHER THE COFFIN LID IS CURSED OR NOT. BUT IF YOU'RE EVER IN LONDON, STOP BY AND SEE FOR YOURSELF!

OTHER FAMOUS CURSES

HOPE DIAMOND

The Hope diamond is one of the most famous—and most cursed—gems in the world. Many people who have owned or worn it have come to tragic ends. King Louis XIV of France died of a horrible infection. King Louis XVI and Marie Antoinette both had their heads cut off. In the 1900s, the diamond's owner died with his family in a carriage accident. In the 1930s, Evalyn McLean lost her son, daughter, mother-in-law, and husband.

ÖTZI THE ICEMAN

In September 1991, a German couple found the mummified remains of a hunter frozen on an icy mountain. Ötzi, as the man came to be called, was more than 5,000 years old! Soon, people who crossed paths with this ancient man started to die tragically. The man who found him froze to death. A scientist who examined the body died suddenly. So did a photographer who made a movie about Ötzi. Should we have left Ötzi where he was?

GLOSSARY

afterlife the life of a person after he or she dies

artifacts the physical remains of an old object

coffins boxes in which people are buried

consulted asked for help from an expert

journalist a writer who works for a news organization

linen a type of cloth woven from a plant

mediums people through whom others seek to communicate with spirits of the dead

pharaohs ancient Egyptian rulers

preserved treated in a way that lets something survive for a long time

spirits supernatural beings, such as ghosts

telegram a message that was sent over a long distance through wires, using electrical signals

tombs buildings in which people are buried

INDEX

Amen-Ra 8, 21
Blavatsky, Madame 14
British Museum 6–7, 18, 21
Cairo 9, 13
Egypt 4–5, 8–10, 13
Hope diamond 22
Johnson, Dr. 18–19
journalist 15
London, England 6, 10, 13, 20–21
mummies 4–5, 7, 9, 18, 20, 22
Murray, Thomas 9–14, 18
Ötzi 22
photographer 17–18
princess 5, 8, 10, 16–17, 20–21
Stead, W. T. 20
Titanic 20
tombs 5, 7–8

READ MORE

Hoena, B. A. *The Mummy's Curse: Discovering King Tut's Tomb (Paranormal Mysteries).* Minneapolis: Bellwether Media, 2020.

Mummies: Riveting Reads for Curious Kids (Mega Bites). New York: DK Publishing, 2020.

Wible-Freels, Korynn. *Ripley Readers Mummies.* Orlando: Ripley Publishing, 2020.

LEARN MORE ONLINE

1. Go to **www.factsurfer.com**
2. Enter "**Egyptian Princess**" into the search box.
3. Click on the cover of this book to see a list of websites.

WITHDRAWN